This book belongs to

_____

_____

For my brothers Adam and Ben ...
and also for Stephen and Chris, who, like the ants,
carry food off Claire's plate and mine!

G.R.

This edition published by Parragon Books Ltd in 2014 and distributed by

Parragon Inc.
440 Park Avenue South, 13th Floor
New York, NY 10016
www.parragon.com

Text and Illustrations © Gemma Raynor 2013

ISBN 978-1-4723-4602-5
Printed in China

Anthony and the Ants

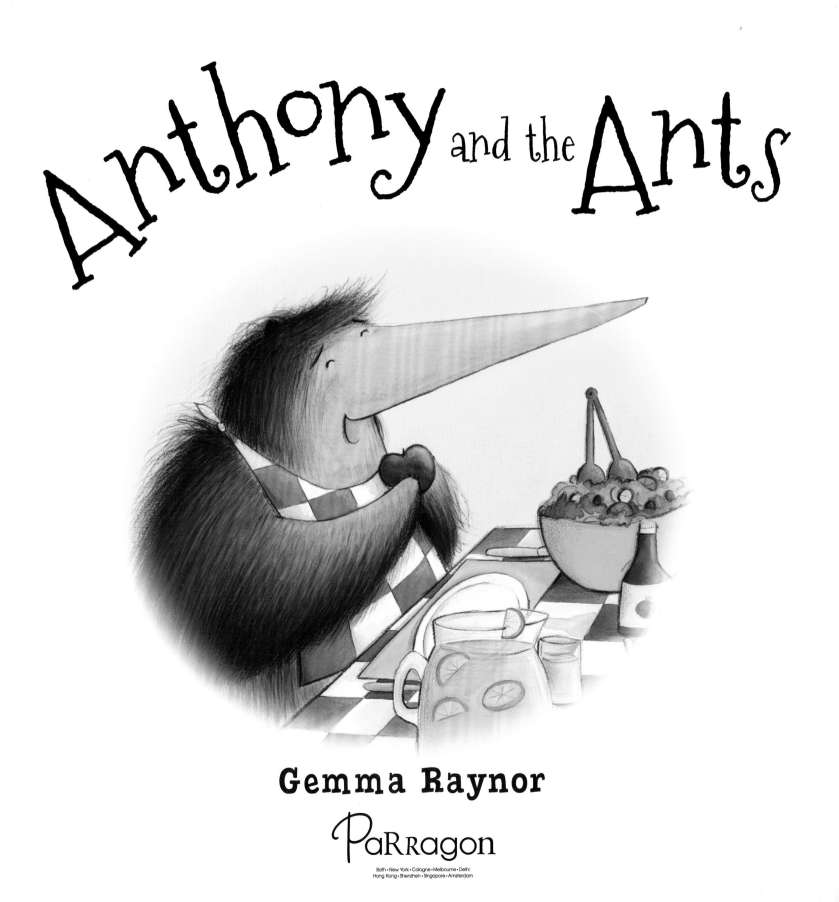

Gemma Raynor

PaRragon

Bath · New York · Cologne · Melbourne · Delhi
Hong Kong · Shenzhen · Singapore · Amsterdam

This is what happened at **breakfast** today—

Anthony's food walked away!

And sadly, that was not the end of that ...

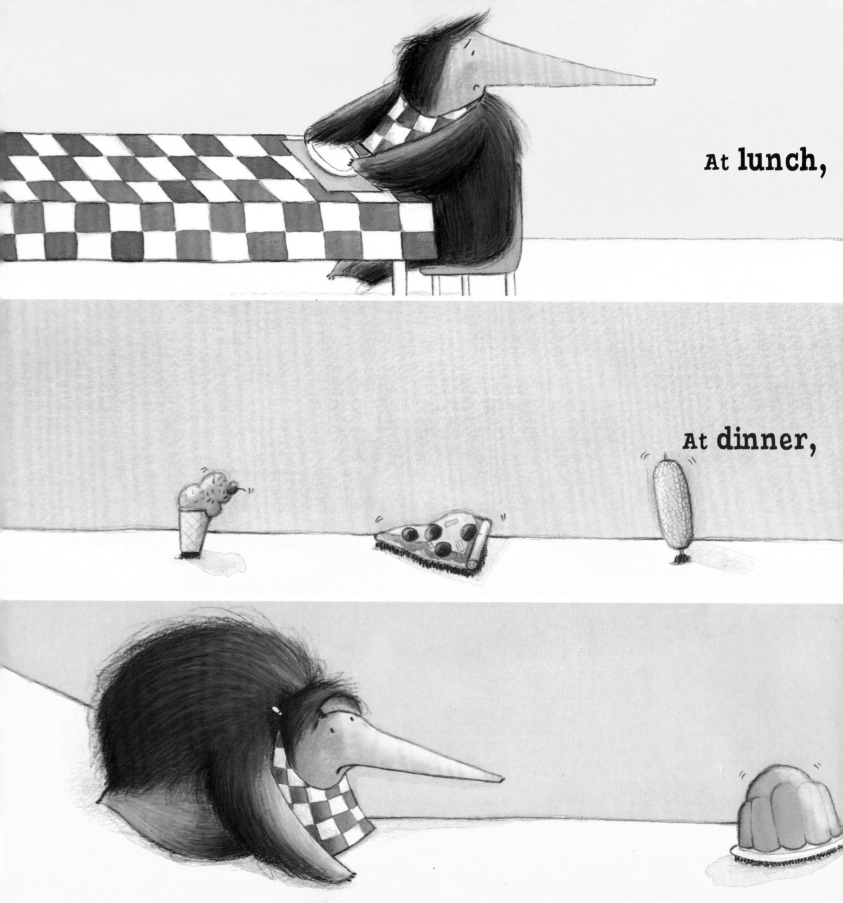

At lunch,

At dinner,

his food leapt from the table.

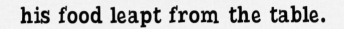

it dashed down the hall.

"Oh what could it be?" poor Anthony cried ...

Ants!

Cheeky ...

Every time Anthony opened his mouth ...

his food had been **carried away!**

Anthony could take no more ...

Snatching an apple, he ran for the door.

Off he sped and up he flew ...

far away to somewhere new.

"I JUST WANT TO EAT THIS APPLE IN PEACE.

Perfect!"

"I agree ..."

said a
BIG HUNGRY BEAR!
"A PERFECT time
for you to drop by!"

And he opened his mouth ...

as wide as could be ...

then all of a sudden, his breakfast was

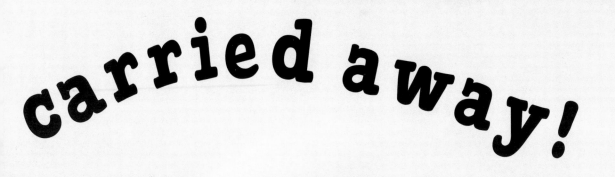

carried away!

By ants, of course,
small, brave, and strong!

Now will everyone FINALLY get along?